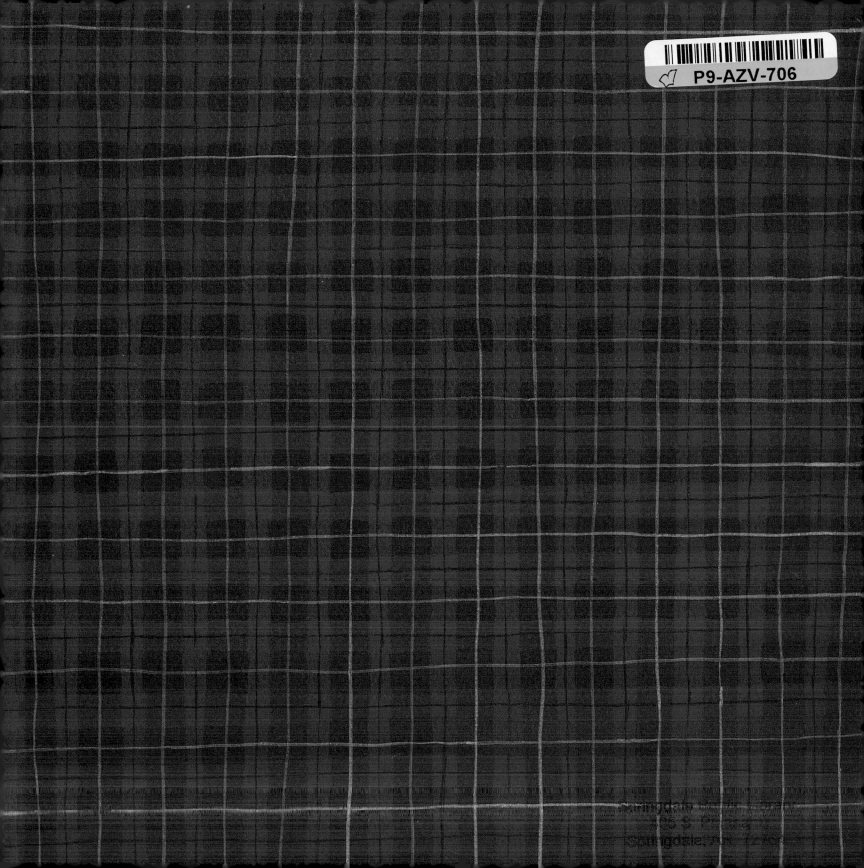

JILL McELMURRY

MAD PLAID
ABOUT

Houghton Mifflin Harcourt

Boston   New York

To Norma Fae

The text type was set in Futura Round.
The display type was set in Populaire.

Library of Congress Cataloging-in-Publication Data is on file.

ISBN: 978-0-358-17244-4

Manufactured in China
SCP 10 9 8 7 6 5 4 3 2 1
4500792223

Madison Pratt found a purse in the park.
It was little and lonely and plaid.

"Poor thing!" she said, and popped the little purse open.

The lonely purse was empty.
It was lined with a sad shade of blue.
"Don't worry," said Madison,
"I'll take care of you."

Madison twirled the little plaid purse in time to the beat of her feet.

PIDDLY-DIDDLY-Doo!

She sang a silly song as she skipped along.

In the middle of a skip, she stopped.

She felt dizzy and frizzled and dazed.

Her fingers tingled.
Her thumbs were hot.
Her arm started twitching and itching a lot.
Then the plaid from the purse crept slowly up her sleeve!

It crawled all over her jacket.

It slithered under her hat.

The plaid did a dance on her underpants.

She cried fat plaid tears all the way home.

Madison scrubbed in the tub
until her skin was sore from rubbing.
But the plaid didn't fade.
In fact, it started to glow.

Her mom flew into a panic
(even though she was a nurse).
She looked in a book called
How to Cure a Plaid Curse.

Sit still.
Be quiet.
Eat a special low-plaid diet.
No kissing or hugging.
Don't use the phone.
Don't belch.
Don't burp.
Don't moan and groan.
Don't laugh or cry.
Don't lose your head.
It lasts a week.

. . . the little book said.

Madison sat very still.
She drank plaid-free cola with careful sips.
But a little plaid burp escaped her lips

and bounced around the room.

OOPS!

It floated around from place to place.
Truly, it was madness!
Everything the plaid germ touched
caught a terrible case of plaidness.

The grocery store and galleries,
the oak trees and the squirrels,
the clouds that rain, the clacking trains,
the ladies and their pearls . . .

the classrooms and the bathrooms,
the buildings tall and small,
the cars and trucks and taxicabs—
the plaidness touched them all!

FAKE FUR POSES REAL

OTHER PATTERN WAITING

MILLIONAIRE OFFERS REWARD FOR PLAID CURE THAT WORKS

VIRUS

POOR MITZI

DON'T PANIC!

OVER 1000 COPIES SOLD
"HOW TO CURE A PLAID CURSE"

DAILY SUN

GOVERNOR DETERMINED UNFIT FOR OFFICE

PLAID IS REAL

NO HOAX

GOVE[RNOR] DECLARES PLAID A HOAX

"PLAID RUINED MY WIFE!" MAN CRIE[S]

PLAID ATTACK

STAR ID

WHEN WILL IT END?

"I MISS MY FLORAL COUCH" SAYS MRS. SMITH

JUST SAY NO TO PLAID

MAD FOR PLAID!

EVENING STAR

SOME ACCUSE SCOTS OF SPREAD[ING] PLAID VIRU[S]

PLAID SPREADS!

Madison saw it on TV.
"Ai-yi-yi, it's getting worse!
I'd better go and get that purse,"
she said, and raced toward the park.

INDEPENDENT

PLAID GOES APE

WORLD GOING PLAID

PLAID DISASTER

PLAID ALL OVER

GARDEN OF PLAID

GLOBE

IT'S A PLAID, PLAID, PLAID, PLAID WORLD

PLAID BE GONE

PLAID

She found the purse alone in the dark.
"You're not to blame for this," she said,
and gave it a little plaid kiss.
"Together, we must reverse this plaidening curse!"

Madison popped the purse open,
remembering the sad shade of blue.

"We've had enough plaid, without a doubt."
So she turned the little purse inside out.

Her fingers tingled.

Her thumbs were hot.

Her arm started twitching and itching a lot.

Then the blue from the purse crept slowly up her sleeve!

The grocery stores and galleries,
the oak trees and the squirrels,
the clouds that rain,
the clacking trains,
the ladies and their pearls . . .
the classrooms and the bathrooms,
the buildings old and new,
the cars and trucks and taxicabs . . .
all turned a sad shade of blue.

But Madison laughed, "Never fear!
I know how to cure the blues."
And then she sang an extra-silly round
of *"Piddly-diddly-doo"*s!

The silliness spread from place to place.

Everything, once sad and grim,
now came alive with a wonderful grin.
(And as you probably already knew,
with a silly grin on, you CAN'T stay blue!)

Madison said to her purse,
"Between you and me,
it could have been worse.

I miss that plaid a little bit.
I'd like to keep some if I may
to have around on any day . . ."

"I'm in a plaidish mood."